TITANIC

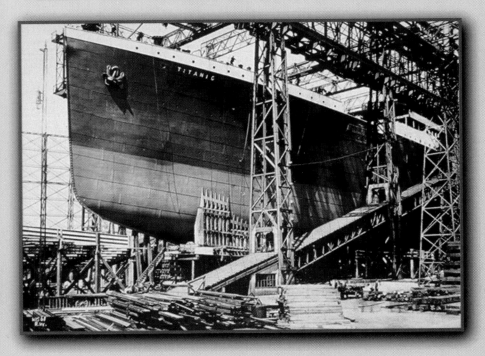

Victoria Sherrow

SCHOLASTIC
REFERENCE

PHOTO CREDITS:
COVER: Front panel: Ralph White/Corbis; back panel: Photograph from "Titanic Survivor" by Violet Jessop, used by permission from Sheridan House, Inc., 1997. Page 1: Ralph White/Corbis; 3: Christie's Images/Corbis; 4: Hulton-Deutsch Collection/Corbis; 6: North Wind; 7: Christie's Images/Corbis; 8: Ralph White/Corbis; 9: Titanic Historical Society, Inc.; 10: AP/Wide World Photos; 11: Fr. Browne S.J. Collection; 12: Titanic Historical Society, Inc.; 13: Bettmann/Corbis; 14: Ken Marschall Collection; 16: ©Museum of the City of New York, Byron Collection; 17: Photograph from "Titanic Survivor" by Violet Jessop, used by permission from Sheridan House, Inc., 1997; 19 (top): Illustrated London News Picture Library; 19 (bottom), Ralph White/Corbis; 21: Bettmann/Corbis; 22: Titanic Historical Society, Inc.; 23: Ulster Folk & Transport Museum; 24:Bettmann/Corbis; 26: Illustrated London News Picture Library; 27: Hulton-Deutsch Collection/Corbis; 29: Titanic Historical Society, Inc.; 30: Illustration by Ken Marschall © 1996 from *I Was There: On Board The* Titanic, a Hyperion/Madison Press Book; 31: Illustrated London News Picture Library; 32: Ralph White/Corbis; 34–35: AP/ Wide World Photos; 36: Bettmann/Corbis; 37: Fr. Browne S.J. Collection; 38: University of Pennsylvania Archives; 40: Ralph White/Corbis; 41: Woods Hole Oceanographic Institute; 42: Underwood & Underwood/Corbis; 43: Titanic Historical Society, Inc.; 44: Bettmann/Corbis.

ISBN 0-439-26706-4

Book design by Kristina Albertson and Nancy Sabato
Photo research by Sarah Longacre

10 9 8 7 6 5 4 3   01 02 03 04

Printed in the U.S.A.   23

First printing, September 2001

We are grateful to Francie Alexander, reading specialist, and to Adele Brodkin, Ph.D., developmental psychologist, for their contributions to the development of this series.

Our thanks also to our history consultant Karen B. Kamuda, Vice-President, the Titanic Historical Society, Inc.

CONTENTS

BIGGER AND BETTER

An excited crowd gathered at the port of Southampton, England, on April 10, 1912. They had come to see a famous new ship. The *Titanic* was the largest vessel ever to set sail. The rooms inside were so grand that people called it a "floating palace." Now the ship was ready for its first trip across the Atlantic Ocean to New York.

What a sight it was! The *Titanic* measured 882 feet (270 meters) from front to back. That is almost as long as four city blocks. The ship rose as tall as an eleven-story building. Its four huge smokestacks soared toward the clouds.

It had taken the White Star company three years to build the *Titanic*. The people who designed the ship wanted it to be extra safe. Its steel **hull** was two layers thick instead of one. The sixteen **compartments** inside the hull had heavy, **watertight** doors. The captain could shut them with a switch in case of an accident. These doors were supposed to keep seawater out of the compartments. The ship could stay afloat even if four compartments filled with water. Some people called the *Titanic* "unsinkable."

The White Star company was proud of its newest ship. In those days, steamship travel was a big business. Steamers carried mail and passengers. Each year, many thousands of people crossed the Atlantic Ocean. Some of these people were going on vacation or to visit friends and family. Most of them crossed the ocean to start new lives in North America.

Steamship companies competed for passengers. Other companies had fine ships, some of which were even faster than the White Star ships. White Star had decided that *their* company would build the biggest and most comfortable ships of all, ships like the *Titanic*.

The Grand Staircase

The passengers who boarded the *Titanic* felt lucky to be on such an impressive ship. Around noon, the whistles blew. Some people took pictures as the giant ship glided down the dock. The passengers waved to people onshore.

Eva Hart and her parents were passengers on the Titanic.

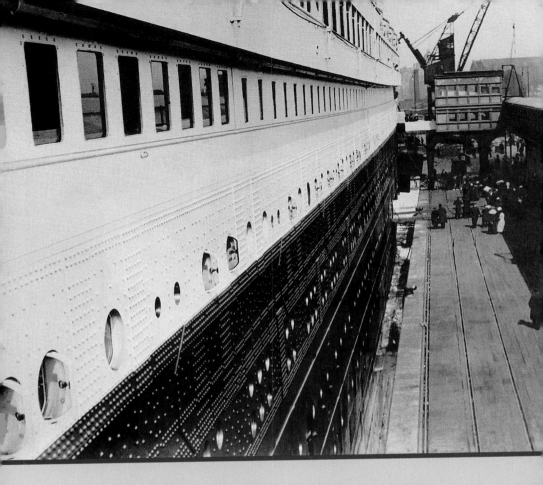

Many of these travelers were wealthy people with first-class tickets. Their tickets cost more than most crewmembers earned in a whole year. First-class passengers brought along servants and heaps of luggage. One family was bringing a new car back home.

Twelve-year-old RUTH BECKER was eager to explore the ship. She was traveling second-class with her mother and younger brother and sister. Their tickets cost less than those for first-class passengers. Ruth was thrilled to see the swimming pool and the Grand Staircase in the first-class dining room. She later wrote, "We were just dazzled when we got on this big lovely boat. . . . Our cabin was just like a hotel room. . . ." Once at sea, Ruth enjoyed watching the seagulls and walking on the long decks.

More passengers joined the ship in France. The last group boarded in Ireland. Most of them had never been on a ship before. They were poor emigrants leaving their homelands. These passengers spoke many languages—Italian, Swedish, German, Polish, French, and Chinese.

In all, 2,208 passengers and crew sailed on the *Titanic*. The green shore of Ireland faded from sight as they steamed out to sea. The *Titanic* was on its way! The ship's captain, Edward J. Smith, said they would reach New York City in six days. During those six days, the passengers expected to have a wonderful time.

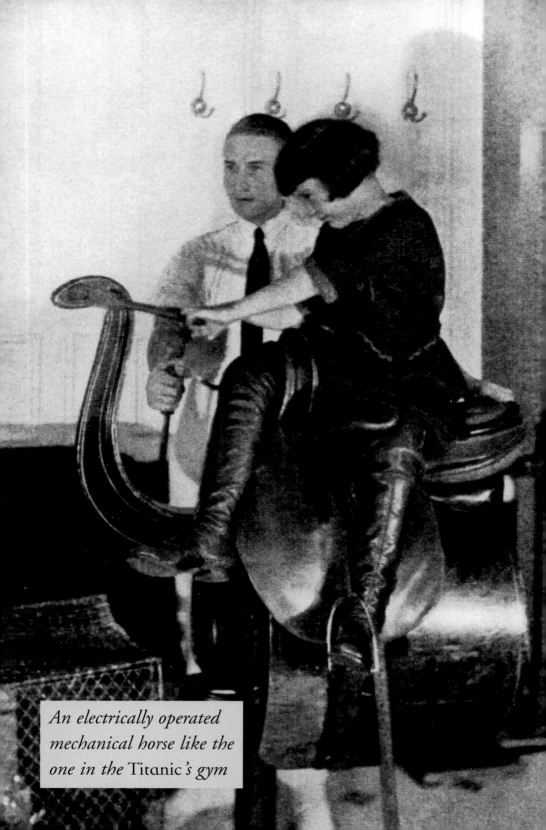

An electrically operated mechanical horse like the one in the Titanic's gym

CHAPTER TWO

A FLOATING HOTEL

Just walking around the *Titanic* was an adventure. The ship had miles (kilometers) of decks and hallways. Passengers used maps to find their way.

First-class passengers could admire large rooms with thick carpets and fancy furniture. Fine paintings and other ornaments hung on the walls. They had their own library, swimming pool, and gym. Children were eager to ride on the exercise "camel" and "horse" that moved up and down.

Second-class rooms were plainer but still very nice. These passengers had their own dining room, library, and deck for sitting or walking.

Third-class passengers paid the lowest prices of all for their tickets. They shared rooms in the lowest part of the ship. This area was called **steerage**. The rooms were small but clean and comfortable. There was also a big room where people could sit, dance, and listen to music.

A second-class room, just like the Becker family's

VIOLET JESSOP was one of the busy crewmembers on the *Titanic*. Stewardess Jessop took care of first-class cabins and passengers. Each day, she carried trays of food for breakfast, tea, and other meals. She made beds and cleaned bathrooms, then vacuumed, swept, and  dusted. Passengers asked her to run errands. At night, she cleaned the rooms again and turned down the beds. Sometimes she had to stay and calm seasick passengers before she went to bed herself.

Hundreds of crew members ran the ship and served the passengers. Mealtimes were especially busy. The ship carried huge amounts of food when it set sail. There were 40,000 eggs; 36,000 apples; 36,000 oranges; 75,000 pounds (34,019 kilograms) of meat; 80,000 pounds (36,287 kilograms) of potatoes; and 1,750 quarts (1,656 liters) of ice cream.

By Saturday afternoon, the *Titanic* was halfway across the Atlantic. J. Bruce Ismay, the head of the White Star company, was on board. He was impressed with the ship's speedy progress. Captain Smith said the *Titanic* would arrive in New York right on time.

The *Titanic* sped across the calm sea under clear skies. People were delighted that the ship was so quiet. One passenger said it was as "firm as a rock."

Sunday, April 14, 1912, was a peaceful day aboard ship. Many went to a church service that morning. The air had turned cold so most people stayed inside. After dinner, people listened to music. Some played card games, read, or talked with friends. By 11:30 P.M., most had gone to bed.

J. Bruce Ismay

Captain Smith

Up in the **crow's nest**, lookouts watched for ships and icebergs. Icebergs often float around the North Atlantic in the spring. Warmer temperatures cause pieces of ice to break away from large glaciers farther north. These chunks of ice can be huge, weighing several thousands of pounds (kilograms). Icebergs can also be miles (kilometers) long and hundreds of feet (meters) tall. It is often difficult to see icebergs at night.

Other ships had passed this way earlier that day. They had seen many icebergs in the water. Their radio operators sent warnings to the *Titanic*. Captain Smith had seen only some of these messages. He did urge the crew to watch out for ice. But Smith did not reduce the speed of the ship or decide to rest in the water until morning.

Suddenly, the lookout spotted something in the dark water. "Iceberg right ahead!" he yelled. He rang a bell in warning.

Quickly, the crew tried to steer away from the iceberg. The front of the ship missed hitting it. But sharp pieces of ice scraped the ship's side. Water rushed into several compartments before the watertight doors could be shut.

Many photographers claimed to have taken pictures of the iceberg that sank the Titanic. *This is one.*

Men working in the boiler room of a ship like the Titanic

Many passengers heard nothing. Others heard a slight noise and felt a jolt. Men working in the engine rooms heard a crunching noise. Some third-class passengers found chunks of ice on the lower decks.

Captain Smith spoke with Thomas Andrews, who had been in charge of the team that built the *Titanic*. Andrews was on board for this first voyage on the new ship.

Andrews and the ship's carpenter rushed to check the damage. They saw that water had already filled five compartments. Andrews said the ship was going to sink. It would go down in less than two hours.

Thomas Andrews supervised the building of the Titanic.

Passengers hardly noticed the ship's lifeboats until disaster struck.

CHAPTER THREE

DISASTER!

Captain Smith told his crew the terrible news: They would have to get the passengers ready to abandon ship. But they must try not to upset people.

The crew moved throughout the ship. They told the passengers to dress warmly and put on their **life jackets**. The crew did not tell them the ship was doomed.

BRAVE AS THE "BIRKENHEAD" BAND: THE "TITANIC'S" MUSICIAN HEROES.

The lifeboats were stored on the ship's top deck. First- and second-class passengers were closer to this deck than third-class passengers. People began walking toward the lifeboats. The ship's band tried to help by playing cheerful music.

Crewmen began loading the lifeboats. "Women and children first!" they said. Many passengers did not want to get in. The sea far below them was cold and dark. They wondered how those tiny boats could be as safe as the big ship. Some women also did not want to leave their husbands. The first lifeboats were not full when the crew lowered them into the water.

Meanwhile, the *Titanic*'s radiomen sent repeated calls for help. They used Morse code to tap out the letters "S.O.S." Morse code uses short taps (dots) and long taps (dashes) to form each letter of the alphabet. The men also tapped out "C.Q.D." It means, "Stand by . . . Danger!" Some ships heard these messages. But they were too far away. The *Carpathia* was 58 miles (93 kilometers) to the south. Its captain told his crew to head for the *Titanic*.

By 1:30 A.M., passengers could see that their ship was sinking. The front dipped into the water. Frightened people moved toward the back of the ship.

By 2:05 A.M., only one lifeboat was left. Hundreds of people were still on board. Most of them were men. But many women and children from third-class also stood waiting. The huge ship had sailed with just 20 lifeboats—not nearly enough for everyone.

The lights faded. The *Titanic* leaned deeper into the water. People prayed. Some of them jumped into the freezing sea. Only a few of those who jumped reached the lifeboats. Soon, icicles clung to their hair and clothing.

A life jacket from the Titanic

There are no photographs of the Titanic *going down. This painting shows how it might have looked.*

Before the ship sank, it stood nearly straight up and down. Sparks flashed. People heard crashing noises and a loud roar. Then the ship disappeared.

It didn't seem possible. The mighty *Titanic*, the finest ship in the world, had sunk on its very first voyage.

The survivors sat shivering and scared in their lifeboats. Some wept. Toward dawn, the wind began to stir. Thirty men were especially worried. They stood on a lifeboat that was floating upside down. Would anyone find them before it was too late?

CAPTAIN EDWARD J. SMITH had been at sea for more than forty years when he took charge of the *Titanic*. The friendly, popular captain planned to retire when the trip ended. While the ship was sinking, the captain told his crew, "You can do no more. Abandon your post. Now it's every man for himself." Captain Smith went down with his ship.

A lifeboat with survivors approaches the Carpathia.

CHAPTER FOUR

ASKING WHY

By 4:00 A.M., the lifeboats had been at sea for hours. At last, people saw lights coming toward them. The steamer *Carpathia* had reached the ice-filled waters.

The survivors waved and shouted. The ship's crew helped them aboard and gave them blankets and hot drinks. Doctors on the ship treated the sick and injured. Other passengers on the *Carpathia* helped, too.

Some survivors sat silently or wept. Others looked for their families. Ruth Becker found her mother and brother. They had been sent to a different lifeboat.

People all over the world were shocked to hear that the *Titanic* had sunk. Only 705 people out of 2,208 passengers and crew were saved.

Why had the ship gone down? they asked.
Why had so many died?

New Yorkers wait for news of the Titanic *disaster.*

Both the British and the Americans studied the tragedy. They said the *Titanic* had been going too fast. The captain should have been more careful because of the ice, and he should have held lifeboat drills. They also said many third-class passengers were warned of danger after the other passengers.

J. Bruce Ismay, one of the survivors, provided information about the sinking of the Titanic.

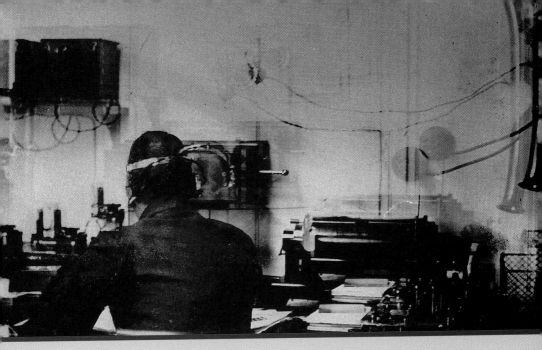

The Titanic's *radio room*

The International Convention for Safety of Life at Sea met in London in 1913 and 1914. New laws were passed to make sea travel safer. All ships had to carry enough lifeboats for all the passengers and crew on board. Crews must be trained to use the lifeboats. Each ship must also have a two-way radio. They must keep it running day and night.

Seventeen-year-old JACK THAYER was glad to see New York Harbor. While the ship was sinking, he had jumped into the sea. He reached the upside-down lifeboat along with more  than twenty other men. Later, Thayer and his mother both made statements about the tragedy to the U.S. Senate. Thayer said the ship had broken in two pieces as it sank.

The International Ice Patrol was set up to keep watch in the North Atlantic. To this day, the ice patrol warns ships about icebergs in the region.

★　★　★

Through the years, people searched for the wreck of the *Titanic*. They could not find the place where the ruined ship had finally settled on the ocean floor. Then, in 1985, a team of scientists spotted the wreckage. It lay more than 2 miles (3 kilometers) underwater. Amazing new tools let scientists find and photograph the ship.

The wreckage lay in two pieces. Jack Thayer and some other survivors had said the *Titanic* broke in two when it sank. Now, scientists saw that these people had been right.

In 1986, scientists explored the wreckage itself. Three men went down in a small submarine. They used a robot to take thousands of amazing color pictures.

One of the Titanic's *propellers, found on the ocean floor*

One of the leaders of this group was Dr. Robert Ballard. Ballard is a world-famous **marine geologist**. He said people should respect the shipwreck as a grave for those who died. It should stay quiet and peaceful in their memory.

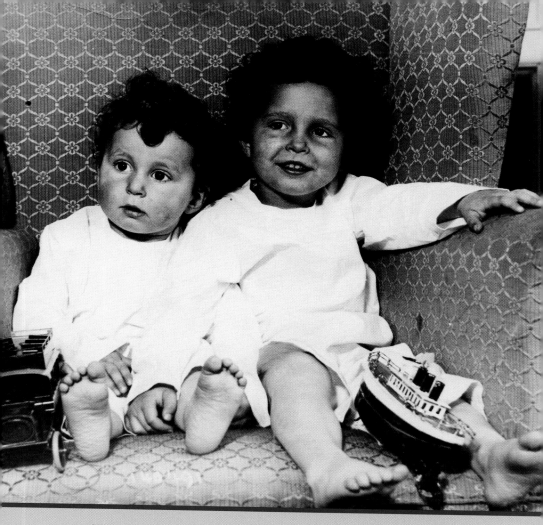

Two survivors of the disaster, aboard a rescue ship

The people who escaped from the *Titanic* never forgot it. Their stories have been told often in books, plays, and movies.

Some survivors talked about their experiences. Others did not. Ruth Becker, who was twelve at the time of the disaster, did not speak about the *Titanic* until she was over sixty years old.

The *Titanic* remains the most famous ship in history. There has never been a worse disaster involving a large ocean liner at sea during peacetime. The story of this fallen ship is one of human mistakes and terrible loss. But it is also a story of great strength and courage.

CHRONOLOGY

1909	White Star company begins building the *Titanic*.
May 31, 1911	The *Titanic* is launched.
April 10, 1912	The *Titanic* leaves from the port at Southampton, England, on its first trip.
April 14, 1912	At 11:40 P.M., the ship strikes an iceberg. Radio operators send out calls for help.
April 15, 1912	The ship sinks at about 2:10 A.M.
April 15, 1912	The ship *Carpathia* arrives at about 4:10 A.M. and takes survivors on board.
April 18, 1912	Survivors reach New York aboard the *Carpathia*.
April 19–May 25, 1912	The U.S. Senate investigates the tragedy.
May 3–July 3, 1912	The British Board of Trade investigates the sinking of the *Titanic*.
May 28, 1912	American investigators report their findings.
November 1913 and January 1914	The International Convention for Safety of Life at Sea meets in London.
1914	The International Ice Patrol is formed.
1985	American and French scientists find the wreckage of the *Titanic*.
1986	Dr. Robert Ballard and two other scientists explore the *Titanic*.

compartments—separate sections inside the body of the ship

crow's nest—a platform high on the ship's mast where the lookout keeps watch

hull—the frame or body of the ship

life jackets—garments worn to keep people afloat in the water

marine geologist—a scientist who studies the structure and history of the earth below the seas

steerage—the section of the ship that holds third-class rooms

watertight—built so tightly that water cannot enter or escape

★ ★ ★ INDEX ★ ★ ★

NOTE TO PARENTS ✦ ✦ ✦

A whole world of discovery opens for children once they begin to read. Illustrated stories and chapter books are wonderful fun for children, but it is just as important to introduce your son or daughter to the world of nonfiction. The ability to read and comprehend factual material is essential for all children, both in school and throughout life.

History is full of fascinating people and places. Scholastic History Readers™ feature clear texts and wonderful photographs of real-life adventures from days gone by.

✦ ✦ ✦ FOR FURTHER READING ✦ ✦ ✦

ADAMS, SIMON. *Eyewitness: Titanic.*
New York: Dorling Kindersley, 1999.

BALLARD, ROBERT. *Exploring the Titanic.*
New York: Scholastic, 1993.

BREWSTER, HUGH, AND LAURIE COULTER.
*882 ½ Amazing Answers to Your
Questions About the Titanic.*
New York: Scholastic, 1999.

MCKEOWN, ARTHUR. *Titanic.*
New York: Aladdin, 1998.